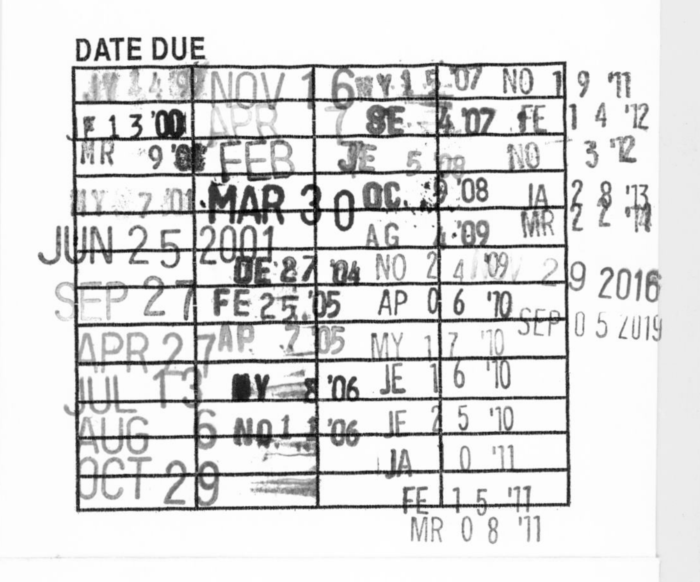

Three Yellow Dogs

by Caron Lee Cohen
pictures by Peter Sis

Greenwillow Books, New York

The preseparated art was printed in four colors.
The typeface is Futura Book.

105 Madison Avenue, New York, N.Y. 10016. Printed in the United States of America
First Edition 10 9 8 7 6 5 4 3 2 1

Library of Congress Cataloging-in-Publication Data

Cohen, Caron Lee.
Three yellow dogs.
Summary: Describes, with only five different words in the text, the adventures of three yellow dogs.
[1. Dogs—Fiction] I. Sis, Peter, ill.
II. Title. PZ7.C65974Th 1986
[E] 85-24823
ISBN 0-688-06230-X
ISBN 0688-06231-8 (lib. bdg.)

FOR LIBBY

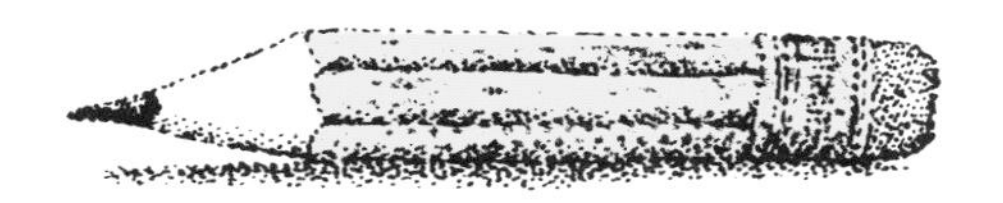

dogs

SCHOOL BUS

yellow

yellow dogs

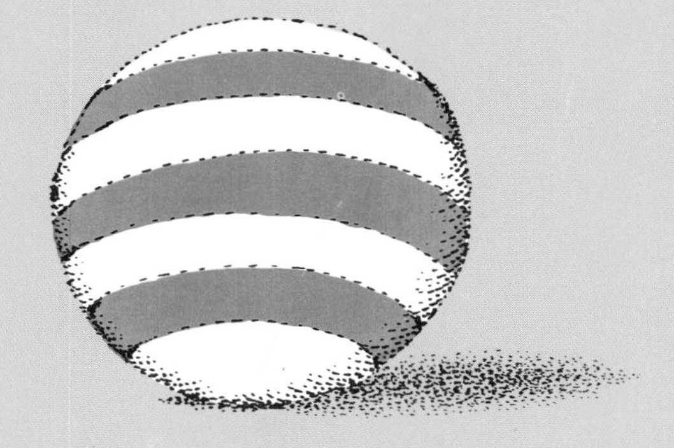

three

three dogs

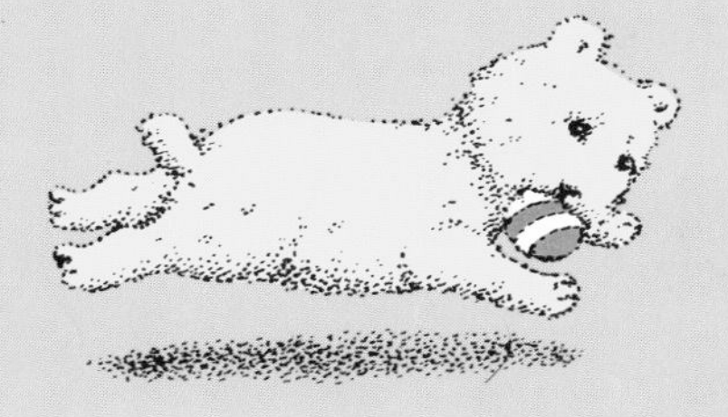

three yellow dogs

home

yellow home

Run.

Run home.

Dogs run.

Yellow dogs run.

Run yellow dogs!

Dogs run home.

Run home dogs!

Three yellow dogs run.

Yellow dogs run home.

Run home

yellow dogs!

Three yellow dogs

run home.